OLIVE & ROGER

HOMER

NUGGET

DAZZLE

BANJO

IVY

LILYANNA

PIPER

Book  Buddies

Marco Polo
Brave Explorer

Cynthia Lord

illustrated by
Stephanie Graegin

CANDLEWICK PRESS

Text copyright © 2022 by Cynthia Lord
Illustrations copyright © 2022 by Stephanie Graegin

First edition 2022

Library of Congress Catalog Card Number 2021946945
ISBN 978-1-5362-1355-3

21 22 23 24 25 26 LBM 10 9 8 7 6 5 4 3 2 1

Printed in Melrose Park, IL, USA

This book was typeset in Sabon.
The illustrations were created digitally.

Candlewick Press
99 Dover Street
Somerville, Massachusetts 02144

www.candlewick.com

A JUNIOR LIBRARY GUILD SELECTION

To Sarah
CL

For Sophia and Olivia
SG

CHAPTER ONE
Marco Polo

Marco Polo was a mouse Christmas ornament. He was small enough to fit in a pocket and made of soft felt. His tail and arms had wire inside and could be bent to hold things or curled to dangle from a finger or a coat hook.

He wore a little green vest and an acorn-cap hat. A loop of red ribbon was sewn to the back of his vest so he could hang on a Christmas tree.

He had been made for a favorite librarian named Anne.

"Oh my goodness!" Anne said when she saw him. "This little mouse looks ready for an adventure. I'll name him Marco Polo after another brave explorer."

Marco Polo thought a brave explorer sounded like a good thing to be.

At home, Anne looped Marco Polo's ribbon around a branch of her Christmas tree. Every night he watched the tree lights blink: red, green, yellow, pink, and blue. He listened to the Christmas music and happy laughter when people came to visit.

It was a nice life, but not an exciting one.

It's hard to be a brave explorer when you can't go anywhere, Marco Polo thought.

So Marco Polo used his imagination. The Christmas tree smelled like outdoors. He imagined himself in a forest.

He'd race across the deep snow.

He'd go into the darkest middle of the woods.

Wolves and bears might chase him.

But brave explorers are never afraid!

He was just pretending, though. Marco Polo's ribbon kept him tied to the Christmas tree between a snowman and a Santa ornament.

Then on New Year's Day, Anne brought out a big box. She placed it beside the tree.

Marco Polo was excited. *What could be in the box?*

But when Anne opened it, the box was empty.

Anne lifted the snowman ornament off the branch. She cupped her hand to hold it gently. "See you next Christmas," she said, putting the snowman in the box.

Next Christmas? Marco Polo couldn't believe his tiny ears. *What does she mean?*

Anne lifted Marco Polo off the branch. She smiled, holding him in her hand. "You're so cute. I hate to put you away," she said. "If you were bigger, you could be a Book Buddy at the library. The children would love you." Then she sighed. "But you're too small. I'm afraid you'd get lost."

Anne put Marco Polo into the box with the snowman.

Marco Polo's heart broke. *Too small? Aren't mice* supposed *to be small?*

"But . . ." Anne said slowly.

She thought for a moment. Then she got a pair of scissors.

"Sometimes it's good to take a chance," Anne said. She took Marco Polo out of the box. She cut his ribbon.

"You're not a Christmas ornament anymore," she said, pulling the ribbon from his vest. "You're a Book Buddy."

Marco Polo stared at the curl of red ribbon on the floor. He couldn't believe his tiny eyes.

He was a real toy.

CHAPTER TWO

The Library

At the library, Marco Polo became a Book Buddy. Book Buddies were library toys and stuffed animals that children could read to and borrow. Each Book Buddy even had a journal so the child could write or draw the toy's adventures at their house.

All the children loved Marco Polo. At the library, they read stories to him. His favorite ones were about mice that had adventures. He especially loved stories about Geronimo Stilton,

Stuart Little, Babymouse, and Ralph from *The Mouse and the Motorcycle*.

The children played with him at the library. Sometimes he slept in the dollhouse. Other times, a child built him a mouse-size city with the blocks. The wire in his tail and arms helped him swing from fingers, coat hooks, table edges, and bookshelves.

Being a Book Buddy seemed like a perfect job for a brave explorer, except for one very big problem.

Marco Polo hardly ever left the library.

Most parents never gave him a chance. "Don't pick that one," they'd say. "He's too small. He might get lost."

Marco Polo would go back on the shelf. He'd watch the child choose Homer the owl or Dazzle the unicorn or Olive the hen and her chick, Roger.

The other Book Buddies had journals full of adventures, but Marco Polo's only had a few pages filled.

It's hard to be a brave explorer when you can't go anywhere, Marco Polo thought over and over.

Then one day Seth came to the library with his dad and little brother. Marco Polo liked Seth because he read adventure books. Today Seth wore a blue T-shirt with a cactus on it.

Marco Polo imagined himself in the desert.

He'd run across the hot sand.

He'd eat cactus flowers and sip cactus juice.

Coyotes might chase him. Rattlesnakes might snap their jaws at him.

But brave explorers are never afraid!

"Story time will start in five minutes," Anne called to the parents and children reading in the beanbags and playing games at the little tables. "Today I'm reading stories about chickens. Get ready to cluck! Our first book is *Interrupting Chicken*."

"Nate, you'll love that one!" Seth told his little brother. "It's so funny. I read it when I was little."

"Cluck! Cluck!" said Nate.

Anne smiled at them. "And we can't have a chicken story time without Olive and Roger," she said. "They'll be our guests of honor. Would you boys carry them for me?"

9

Marco Polo saw his chance. *Sometimes brave explorers must take matters into their own paws*, he thought.

Marco Polo hooked his tail into Roger's tag.

Seth picked the black-and-white hen off the Book Buddies shelf. He handed her to his little brother. "You can carry Olive."

Nate made Olive fly by flapping her wings.

Then Seth picked up the fluffy yellow chick. "Come on, Roger."

Marco Polo came, too!

But only for a few seconds.

His tail fell out of Roger's tag, and he tumbled to the floor at Seth's feet.

"Marco Polo, I promise you'll be the guest of honor at a story time soon." Anne set him gently back on the shelf. "Today, it's Roger and Olive's turn."

"Marco Polo is a funny name for a mouse," Seth's dad said.

"I thought he looked like a brave explorer ready for an adventure," Anne said.

"Seth is going on an adventure this weekend!" Dad said proudly. "A birthday party sleepover!"

"Really, Seth?" Anne asked. "That's so exciting! Will this be your first sleepover?"

Seth shrugged. "Nate and I have slept at Grandma and Grandpa's house," he said. "But I've never slept over at a friend's house."

"Lots of kids are coming to Ben's birthday party," Dad said. "But Ben could only pick one friend to sleep over. And he picked Seth!"

"Can I borrow Marco Polo?" Seth asked. "I want to take him on my sleepover."

Yes! A sleepover would be a perfect adventure for a brave explorer! Marco Polo thought.

"I don't know," Dad said. "He's so small. I'm afraid he'll get lost." He picked up Piper the flying squirrel. "How about this one? He's cute, too."

"No thank you," Seth said.

Dad picked up Homer the owl. "Or this one?"

Seth shook his head. "I only want Marco Polo," he said sadly.

Marco Polo felt sad, too.

He watched Seth follow Dad and Nate off to story time. *What does it mean to get lost? Why is everyone afraid of it?*

He wished Seth's dad would give him a chance. He'd prove that being small was not a bad thing.

"Thank goodness they're gone," a voice said. "I've been holding this sneeze in all morning!"

13

CHAPTER THREE

The Book Buddies

Achoo!" Dazzle the unicorn sneezed. Sparkles from his tail floated in the air. "That's the problem with glitter," he said. "Sometimes it goes up my nose."

"It goes up *all* our noses!" Homer the owl complained. "You should have feathers like me. They don't come off and annoy the rest of us."

"I like my glitter," said Dazzle. "And so do the children. I get borrowed a lot because I'm sparkly."

"Me too," said Lilyanna the princess doll, showing off her sparkly dress. "I wonder who will choose me today? Last time I got to go to the beach!"

"I rode in a bicycle basket," Banjo the bear said. "I loved going fast. My fur blew in the wind!"

"I hope I am borrowed with another Book Buddy," Ivy the doll said. "I like having fun with friends."

"I just hope I get chosen by *anyone*," Marco Polo said quietly.

Banjo put a soft paw around Marco Polo. "Seth really wanted you. I think his dad almost said yes."

Piper nodded. "It was really close."

Marco Polo sighed. *Almost* and *close* were terrible words. They got your hopes up. But then they turned into *no*.

"Shh!" said Homer. "I hear the children coming. Everyone get back to your places! And Dazzle, control your glitter!"

As the children rushed into the room, Marco Polo imagined what he wished would happen.

A child would see him from across the room.
"I want Marco Polo!"

"Yes, of course!" the parent would say. "He is the perfect choice!"

And—

Marco Polo was picked up. "Please, Dad?" Seth asked.

Dad sighed. "Are you sure you don't want the bear? He'd be easy to find when it's time to come home."

Seth shook his head. "I only want Marco Polo."

"All right," Dad said. "But it's your job to take care of him."

"I will," Seth promised.

As Dad helped Nate pick out books, Seth carried Marco Polo to the checkout desk. Anne scanned the bar code for Marco Polo's journal.

"Marco Polo's journal is bigger than he is!" Seth said.

Anne smiled. "Brave explorers have big adventures!" she said. "I'll be excited to see what you write and draw in his journal. I know that you and Marco Polo will have a fun time at the sleepover."

Seth peeked to make sure Dad was busy. Then he leaned toward Anne. "I'm a tiny bit worried," he whispered. "What if I have to get up in the middle of the night? Or I hear strange sounds?"

"Do you have a flashlight?" Anne whispered back.

Seth nodded.

"Worrying can be scary," Anne said. "But remember that if something big goes wrong, you can always ask for help. And for little things, I know you'll figure it out."

Seth tucked the journal under his arm. That sounded nice, but it sounded too easy. What if he *couldn't* figure it out? He didn't want to look silly to Ben. Or like a baby to Ben's older brother, Peter.

As he waited for Dad and Nate, Seth whispered into Marco Polo's tiny ear, "You're brave. That's why I need you."

CHAPTER FOUR

Seth

Seth had read the invitation so many times that he knew it by heart.

You are invited to a birthday party!

Inside the invitation, it listed the time and day. At the bottom, Ben had written, *Mom said I can invite one friend to sleep over. I picked you! Can you come? Please say yes!*

Seth loved birthday parties. He liked the cake, balloons, and games. He was happy that

Ben had picked him to sleep over. He had some worries, though.

What if he had a nightmare?

What if he missed Nate and Dad?

What if he had to use the bathroom in the middle of the night?

What if his flashlight rolled away in the dark and he couldn't find it?

And how could he sleep without his stuffed bunny, Boo? Boo had been Seth's favorite toy since he was a baby. A long time ago, Boo had been white. Over the years, her fur had been loved to gray. She even had some places where you could see her stitching. It didn't matter to Seth, though. She was beautiful to him.

Seth slept with Boo every night, sometimes even using Boo's soft tummy for a pillow. When Seth slept over at Grandma and Grandpa's, Boo went, too. Grandma had even made Boo her own blanket.

Seth had never told Ben about Boo, though. What if Ben or Peter made fun of him for sleeping with a stuffed animal? Or even worse, what if they made fun of Boo? What if they said she was old and ugly with her gray fur and stitches showing?

Seth couldn't stand that thought. So when Seth saw Marco Polo at the library, he made a plan.

Marco Polo was small enough to tuck into his sleeping bag without making a big lump. No one would know he was there—except Seth.

Marco Polo wasn't Boo. But knowing he had a tiny, brave secret friend made Seth feel braver, too.

"Hi, Seth!" Ben's mom said as she opened the door. "I'm so glad you could come to the party. You can put your sleeping bag and backpack in Ben and Peter's room."

"I'll show you!" Ben took Seth's backpack.

Dad gave Seth a hug. "I'll pick you up in the morning. You know my phone number. So if you need me you can call me."

"Yes," Ben's mom said. "You can use my phone anytime."

"Thanks." Seth took a deep breath. "Okay! See you tomorrow, Dad!"

Then he picked up his sleeping bag. Seth was glad he had rolled Marco Polo up tightly inside so he wouldn't fall out.

He followed Ben into the party.

CHAPTER FIVE

The Party

At the party, Seth and the other kids blew up balloons and batted them around the room, trying to keep them in the air. They watched Ben open his presents and played with Ben's new birthday toys. They saw a movie about superheroes and ate pizza, ice cream, and Ben's dinosaur cake.

"Benny used to be afraid of T. rexes," Peter said. "Remember? Anything with teeth made you squeal." Peter made a scary face. "Like monsters!"

"I'm not afraid anymore!" Ben said, making a scary face back. "And don't call me Benny."

"Okay, Benny-Penny," Peter teased.

During the daytime, Seth liked that Ben's house was different from his own house. The bathroom had fish wallpaper. Ben and Peter had bunk beds in their room. They even had a pet cat named Tulip.

"My mom named her after a flower," Ben said. "Tulip loves to play, but be careful, because she steals socks!"

Seth decided to keep his socks on, just in case.

But when it was time for bed, Ben's house was a lonely kind of different.

"Good night," Ben's mom said. "Seth, remember I'm right down the hallway. Don't feel shy about waking me up if you need anything tonight. I'll leave a night-light on in the hallway."

Ben's mom tucked in Ben, Peter, and Seth, but it wasn't the same. Seth missed reading Nate a bedtime story. He missed his good-night kiss from Dad and hearing him say, "Good night, sleep tight."

As soon as the door was shut, Peter asked, "Who wants to tell ghost stories?"

"Not me!" Ben said.

Seth was glad he didn't have to say no first. "Me, either," he said.

"You guys are scaredy-cats," Peter said, turning over in bed. "Good night, Benny-Penny. Good night, Sethie-Wethie."

Seth knew Peter was teasing, but he didn't like it. *I'll never tease Nate like that,* he promised himself.

Thinking of Nate made him miss home again.

It took Seth a long time to fall asleep. Even the dark was different at Ben's house. The shadows weren't the same as the shadows at home.

He missed Boo. He missed Dad. He even missed the sound of Nate's quiet breathing. Peter snored.

Seth reached down and pulled Marco Polo out of the sleeping bag. "Good night, sleep tight," he whispered, giving Marco Polo's acorn hat a kiss.

He laid Marco Polo on the pillow next to him where Boo usually slept. *I just have to remember to hide him again in the morning,* Seth thought.

With Marco Polo beside him, Seth finally fell asleep.

He slept so deeply that he didn't hear the door open.

He didn't see two pointy ears and a fluffy tail framed by the hallway night-light.

Marco Polo *did* hear and see them, though. And he knew what they meant.

Trouble.

CHAPTER SIX
Tulip

Marco Polo knew cats could be trouble—even for a toy mouse. *Maybe she won't notice me on Seth's pillow,* he hoped.

Tulip didn't make a sound as she walked into the room. She rubbed her cheek on Seth's backpack, sniffing for snacks or socks to steal.

Then Marco Polo saw two green eyes glowing in the darkness next to the pillow.

She'd seen him.

Tulip's whiskers tickled Marco Polo's face. She reached out her paw. *Swipe!* She batted him off the pillow onto the floor.

Marco Polo felt her teeth close on his tail. Suddenly, he was dangling upside down!

Oh no! Marco Polo thought.

Tulip slipped out of Ben's room with Marco Polo hanging from her teeth. She carried him through the living room.

She carried him through the kitchen.

She pushed open the cat door to the garage.

Moonlight shone onto the garage floor from the windows. It made everything look big and scary. *Drop me near the car,* Marco Polo wished. *Then the family will find me.*

But Tulip sneaked past the car to an old couch. She squeezed herself into the space between the couch and the wall.

Marco Polo couldn't believe his tiny eyes. In the moonlight, he could see a big pile of things.

Hair ties.

Lipstick.

Markers.

Bottle caps.

Straws.

Plastic rings from milk jugs.

A small flashlight.

A gold earring.

And lots of socks!

Tulip dropped Marco Polo onto the pile. Some of the things had dust on them, making Marco Polo sneeze.

Then Tulip curled herself into a ball and closed her eyes.

What if no one ever finds me here behind the couch? Marco Polo thought as Tulip fell asleep. *I might never see Seth again. I might never see my Book Buddy friends again.*

Marco Polo was scared. He was too scared to even pretend to be brave.

"Who are you?" a voice whispered.

CHAPTER SEVEN
A Monster

Marco Polo peered into the shadows. A small green head poked out from under the couch.

The head had horns.

Two big eyes.

A grinning mouth with fangs.

Marco Polo couldn't believe his tiny eyes. *A monster!* He grabbed a straw and swung it in front of him like a sword. "Stand back!"

"Why?" the monster asked.

"Aren't you a monster?" Marco Polo asked.

"Yes," the monster said. "Nice to meet you. I'm Moby."

Marco Polo peered closer. Moby was a monster, but a soft toy one. He was no bigger than Marco Polo himself. "I'm Marco Polo."

"Have you seen Ben?" Moby asked. "He's my boy, and I'm worried about him."

Marco Polo put down the straw. "Yes, it's Ben's birthday. I came with Seth to his party."

"Ben's birthday?" Moby asked. "Oh, please tell me all about it! Was there a cake? How old is Ben now?"

"I don't know how old he is," Marco Polo said. "And I didn't get to see a cake. I was hidden in Seth's sleeping bag. He brought me with him to help him feel braver. But then I got captured."

"Me too." Even Moby's smile looked sad. "Ben is scared of monsters under his bed. So Mom bought me. I'm not scary, but I can speak monster. So I can tell the other monsters to go away."

"Well, you both failed!" A silver-and-red action figure crawled out from under the couch. "And now you'll be stuck here forever. I hope you're quiet, Marco Polo! I'm sick of Moby whining about 'Ben this' and 'Ben that.'"

"This is Ranger," Moby said. "He's been here the longest."

"The kitten brought me here first," Ranger said. "And I was perfectly happy all alone! Then Moby came."

"Kitten?" Marco Polo asked.

Ranger nodded. "Her name is Tulip."

Marco Polo couldn't believe his tiny ears. Tulip was a grown-up cat now. Ranger must've been behind the couch for a long time.

Is this why everyone is so afraid of being lost? Marco Polo wondered. *Because it can take so long to be found again?*

"I have to get back to Seth," Marco Polo said.

"How?" Moby asked.

But Marco Polo had no idea.

"Just face it," Ranger said. "No one will look for you here. You're stuck here forever, so you may as well go to sleep."

Marco Polo couldn't sleep, though. Worrying kept him awake.

What if Ranger is right? What if no one ever finds me?

The nighttime shadows turned everything around him into dark lumps and scary bumps. For the first time, Marco Polo wondered if maybe he should have stayed a Christmas ornament. At least he would've been safe in the box. *Maybe I'm not a brave explorer after all,* Marco Polo thought. *Maybe I'm just a scared, lost little mouse.*

"Are you still awake?" Moby whispered in the dark.

"Yes," Marco Polo said quietly. "I can't sleep."

"Is it monsters?" Moby asked. "I'll scare them away. It's my job."

"No, it's not monsters," Marco Polo said. "I'm lost and alone."

"You're not alone with me," Moby said. "We're together."

Marco Polo hooked his arm around Moby. Holding on to a friend made Marco Polo feel braver.

If no one finds me, I'll have to rescue myself, he thought.

But how?

CHAPTER EIGHT
A Rescue

In the morning, sunlight shone through the garage windows. It took away the nighttime shadows. The dark lumps and scary bumps turned back into hair ties, socks, and other ordinary things.

Behind the couch wasn't a scary place in the daytime. It was just new.

Discovering new places is what explorers do, Marco Polo thought. After all those times he'd imagined himself as a brave explorer, now he could really be one.

Time to take matters into my own paws, he thought. He looked at Tulip, fast asleep. He used his imagination.

He'd found the cat's secret cave.

And her pile of treasure!

The cat might chase him. She might grab him in her teeth.

But brave explorers are never—

Marco Polo stopped. He had been afraid. *But maybe even brave explorers get scared sometimes,* he thought. *Maybe they just keep trying anyway.*

That gave Marco Polo a very brave idea. He didn't know if it would work, but as Anne had said, *Sometimes it's good to take a chance.*

He would escape.

But he wouldn't escape alone.

"Moby, wake up," he whispered. "I have an idea."

Moby yawned. "What?"

"I'm going to escape," Marco Polo said. "And I can hold on to things with my arms and tail. So I can hold on to *you* and take you with me."

"I'll see Ben again!" Moby grinned, but then he added, "But what about Ranger?"

"I'm too heavy," Ranger said, turning around to face them.

Marco Polo knew Ranger was right. Moby was little and easy to hold, but he'd never hold on to Ranger for more than a few seconds. The wire in his arms wasn't strong enough.

"Go on! I'll be fine without you two," Ranger said. "In fact, I'll be great! It will be quiet again, just like it was before you came." Ranger's voice cracked a little, though. "Good luck, Moby. I hope Ben still remembers you."

"Me too," Moby said. "I wish we could tell Ben where to find you, Ranger."

That gave Marco Polo another brave idea. Maybe he couldn't bring Ranger to the children, but could he bring the children here?

Marco Polo looped hair ties and milk jug rings onto one arm.

"What are those for?" Moby whispered.

"A trail," Marco Polo whispered back. He put his other arm around Moby. Then he looked at the sleeping cat. *Here comes the hard part,* he thought.

Marco Polo had used his tail to dangle from fingers, coat hooks, table edges, and bookshelves.

But never from a cat's tail.

CHAPTER NINE

A Surprise

Seth's first thought upon waking was *I did it!* He felt proud that he had slept through the night at Ben's house.

Ben and Peter were still asleep. So Seth's second thought was to hide Marco Polo.

But when Seth touched his pillow, Marco Polo wasn't there.

Seth felt inside his sleeping bag, moving his hand up and down.

Nothing.

Marco Polo wasn't on the floor nearby. He hadn't rolled up against Seth's backpack. *Where is he?*

Seth crawled out of his sleeping bag to look under Ben's dresser.

"What are you doing?" Ben asked from the bottom bunk.

Peter rolled over in the top bunk to look at Seth. "Did you lose something?"

Seth's heart sank. He didn't want Peter and Ben to find Marco Polo. "Um. I think my flashlight might have rolled under here."

"Don't worry," Ben said. "I'll help you look for it."

"No! No, that's okay," Seth said. "I can look myself. I'm sure it just rolled under something."

"I can help." Ben climbed out of bed and started looking, too. "Maybe it's under the heater?"

Peter climbed down the bunk-bed ladder. He picked up Seth's pillow. There was the flashlight.

"It was right here all the time!" Peter said.

Seth didn't know what to do. Then he decided to tell Ben and Peter the truth. Even if they made fun of him. "I'm sorry. I didn't really lose my flashlight. I lost Marco Polo. He's a toy mouse. I borrowed him from the library to help me feel braver."

Ben looked surprised. "Why?"

"It's my first time sleeping over at your house," Seth said. "And I was a little scared. I've only been to your house in the daytime."

"You two really *are* scaredy-cats." Peter laughed.

"Merrrrrrrrrow!" Suddenly the door pushed open and Tulip ran into the room. She raced around and around, like something was chasing her.

Marco Polo was hanging on to her tail.

"Moby!" Ben cried, grabbing the toys off Tulip's tail. "Where have you been? I've missed you so much."

"Moby?" Seth asked.

"It's his monster lovey-dovey," Peter teased.

Ben's face turned red. He hugged the little green monster to his chest. "Mom bought Moby for me because sometimes I get scared in the middle of the night. In the dark, my imagination starts thinking of scary things like monsters. But Moby can speak monster, so he tells the monsters to stay away. It's babyish, right?"

"Yes," Peter said.

"No!" Seth said loudly. "I have a stuffed bunny at home named Boo. I've had her since I was a baby. I wanted to bring her, but I was afraid you might make fun of me."

"I wouldn't do that," Ben said, giving Moby a squeeze. "That's funny. Moby smells like the garage."

Seth looked closely at Marco Polo. There was dust on his acorn-cap hat. "I wonder where they've been."

The boys all looked at Tulip.

"Come on!" Peter said.

CHAPTER TEN

Found Again

The boys followed the trail of milk jug rings and hair ties through the kitchen and into the garage.

The trail went past the car and behind the couch.

"I see something," Peter said. "Help me move the couch."

The boys pulled and pushed until they finally moved the couch away from the wall.

"Look at all the socks!" Ben said. "And there's Mom's earring!"

Peter gasped. "Ranger!" He picked up the action figure. "I lost him a long time ago!"

Ben turned to Tulip. "So this is your hiding place? Now when we lose something, we'll know where to look!"

"I can't believe Ranger has been here the whole time. I thought he was lost forever!" Peter hugged Ranger.

Ben turned to Seth. "Ranger is Peter's lovey-dovey."

"He is not!" Peter said. Then he looked down at Ranger. "I did miss him, though."

Ben crossed his arms. "Just like Seth missed Marco Polo?"

Seth crossed his arms, too. "And Ben missed Moby?"

Peter didn't say anything for a while. Then he sighed. "Well, I guess so," he said quietly. "Maybe you're right."

"What? Say it louder," Ben said.

"Maybe you're right!" Peter said. "I'm sorry I teased you guys about Moby and Marco Polo."

Seth took a deep breath. Peter did seem sorry. So he decided to give Peter another chance. "Okay, but don't call us scaredy-cats or Benny-Penny and Sethie-Wethie anymore."

"I won't," Peter promised. "Maybe we could play with our toys together? I bet they'd like your birthday presents, Benny—" He stopped. "Ben."

"Sure!" Ben said. "Let's play after breakfast. Mom said she'd make pancakes!"

The boys cleaned the dust off the toys. At breakfast, Marco Polo, Moby, and Ranger sat on the table.

Then they rode in Ben's new remote-controlled toy jeep.

They had fun in the modeling clay.

They met dinosaurs.

They looked at comic books.

The boys were having so much fun with Marco Polo, Moby, and Ranger that they didn't even hear the doorbell ring.

"Hi!" Dad said. "How was the sleepover?"

Seth ran to Dad. "I had a great time! And so did Marco Polo. Can we have another sleepover? This time at our house?"

Dad smiled. "Sure!"

"Moby can meet Boo," Ben said.

Seth looked at Peter. "Will you and Ranger come, too?"

Peter smiled. "Yes!"

On the car ride home, Marco Polo was happy. He'd had the biggest adventure of his whole life.

He'd been on a sleepover.

He'd been captured by a cat and escaped.

He'd explored new places and made new friends.

Now he felt excited to go back to the library and see his Book Buddy friends. Because when an adventure is over . . .

Even brave explorers like to go home.

CHAPTER ELEVEN

The Best Part of an Adventure

Seth!" Anne said as soon as she saw him at the library. "How was the sleepover?"

Seth grinned. "It was so much fun! We're having another one in two weeks," he said. "And this time, we're sleeping over at my house!"

"I'm so glad," Anne said.

"There were a few scary things," Seth said. "When it was dark, everything looked different at Ben's house. But the scariest part was that Ben's cat took Marco Polo!"

"Oh no!" Anne said. "What happened?"

Seth opened Marco Polo's journal. He showed Anne the pictures he'd drawn of the sleepover and Marco Polo's new friends.

The last drawing showed Marco Polo meeting Boo at Seth's house.

"That's a lot of adventure for a tiny mouse," Anne said. "In fact, you *both* had an adventure."

Seth nodded. "Can I borrow Marco Polo again for the next sleepover? It wouldn't be the same without him."

Anne smiled. "Of course. I'll reserve him for you."

"I don't need him to help me be brave this time," Seth said. "But he might need to help Ben, Peter, Ranger, and Moby."

"That's what friends do," Anne said. "They help each other."

Marco Polo liked the sound of that! He wanted to see Moby and Ranger again and show them all the fun things in Seth's room—and no cat!

Marco Polo was bursting to tell his Book Buddy friends about his adventures. As soon as Anne and all the children went off to story time, he said, "I went on a sleepover, and a cat came in the middle of the night and stole me right off Seth's pillow."

"Goodness me!" Olive said, covering Roger's ears. "Were you scared?"

Marco Polo nodded. "Then I met an action figure and a monster."

"A monster!" Lilyanna said. "I would've fainted."

"Did the monster have big teeth?" Roger asked.

"Fangs!" Marco Polo said. "But the monster became my friend. His name is Moby."

"Imagine that!" Olive said. "A friendly monster."

Marco Polo nodded. "We escaped because I hung on to the cat's tail."

"That was very brave!" Banjo said.

"I didn't always feel brave," Marco Polo said. "But I learned that even brave explorers get scared sometimes. I had a big adventure, and I discovered something even more important."

All the Book Buddies leaned in close to hear.

"The best part of an adventure is having friends on the adventure with you," Marco Polo said.

And every Book Buddy agreed.

CYNTHIA LORD is the author of award-winning middle-grade fiction titles such as the Newbery Honor Book *Rules, Touch Blue, Half a Chance, A Handful of Stars,* and *Because of the Rabbit.* She is also the author of the Hot Rod Hamster picture book and early reader series as well as the Shelter Pet Squad chapter book series. Cynthia Lord lives in Maine.

STEPHANIE GRAEGIN is the author-illustrator of *Little Fox in the Forest* and the illustrator of many other picture books, including *You Were the First* by Patricia MacLachlan and *Water in the Park* by Emily Jenkins. Stephanie Graegin lives in Brooklyn.

Book  Buddies

Dazzle Makes a Wish

Meet the Book Buddies, toys that can
be checked out from the library,
just like books. For the Book Buddies,
every borrowing is a new adventure!

Welcome to Penguin Young Readers! As parents and educators, you know that each child develops at his or her own pace—in terms of speech, critical thinking, and, of course, reading. Penguin Young Readers recognizes this fact. As a result, each Penguin Young Readers book is assigned a traditional easy-to-read level (1–4) as well as a Guided Reading Level (A–P). Both of these systems will help you choose the right book for your child. Please refer to the back of each book for specific leveling information. Penguin Young Readers features esteemed authors and illustrators, stories about favorite characters, fascinating nonfiction, and more!

Love Is in the Air

LEVEL 2

GUIDED READING LEVEL **H**

This book is perfect for a **Progressing Reader** who:
- can figure out unknown words by using picture and context clues;
- can recognize beginning, middle, and ending sounds;
- can make and confirm predictions about what will happen in the text; and
- can distinguish between fiction and nonfiction.

Here are some **activities** you can do during and after reading this book:
- Picture Clues: Go through the book and match the pictures to the words. For example, point to the picture of Balloon and read the word *balloon* in the story.
- Retelling: What is the story about? What happens at the beginning, middle, and end of the story? Pay close attention to how Balloon is feeling. At first he is lonely, but how does his attitude shift throughout the story?

Remember, sharing the love of reading with a child is the best gift you can give!

—Bonnie Bader, EdM
   Penguin Young Readers program

*Penguin Young Readers are leveled by independent reviewers applying the standards developed by Irene Fountas and Gay Su Pinnell in *Matching Books to Readers: Using Leveled Books in Guided Reading*, Heinemann, 1999.

For Pendy, Coco, and Lulu,
who keep me aloft—JF

Penguin Young Readers
Published by the Penguin Group
Penguin Group (USA) Inc., 375 Hudson Street, New York, New York 10014, USA
Penguin Group (Canada), 90 Eglinton Avenue East, Suite 700, Toronto, Ontario M4P 2Y3, Canada
(a division of Pearson Penguin Canada Inc.)
Penguin Books Ltd., 80 Strand, London WC2R 0RL, England
Penguin Group Ireland, 25 St. Stephen's Green, Dublin 2, Ireland (a division of Penguin Books Ltd.)
Penguin Group (Australia), 250 Camberwell Road, Camberwell, Victoria 3124, Australia
(a division of Pearson Australia Group Pty. Ltd.)
Penguin Books India Pvt. Ltd., 11 Community Centre, Panchsheel Park, New Delhi—110 017, India
Penguin Group (NZ), 67 Apollo Drive, Rosedale, Auckland 0632, New Zealand
(a division of Pearson New Zealand Ltd.)
Penguin Books (South Africa) (Pty.) Ltd., 24 Sturdee Avenue, Rosebank,
Johannesburg 2196, South Africa
Penguin Books Ltd., Registered Offices: 80 Strand, London WC2R 0RL, England

Copyright © 2012 by Jonathan Fenske. All rights reserved. Published by Penguin Young Readers,
an imprint of Penguin Group (USA) Inc., 345 Hudson Street, New York, New York 10014.
Manufactured in China.

Library of Congress Control Number: 2011046785

ISBN 978-0-448-49647-4 (pbk)   10 9 8 7 6 5 4 3
ISBN 978-0-448-46160-1 (hc)   10 9 8 7 6 5 4 3 2 1

LOVE IS IN THE AIR

by Jonathan Fenske

Penguin Young Readers
An Imprint of Penguin Group (USA) Inc.

The cake was gone.

The boys and girls were home.

But Balloon was still tied

to the table.

He was alone.

He started to droop.

5

Then came a gust of wind
and a new friend.

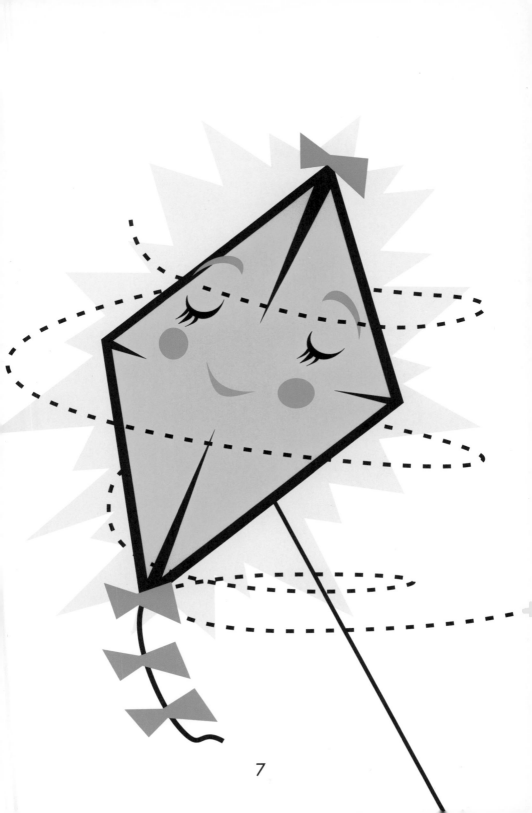

7

Come with me!

said Kite.

She rose on the breeze.

Wait for me!
said Balloon.

He pulled.

And he pulled.

SNAP!

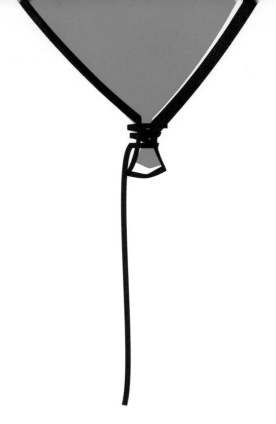

Until he was free.

Hello!

said Kite.

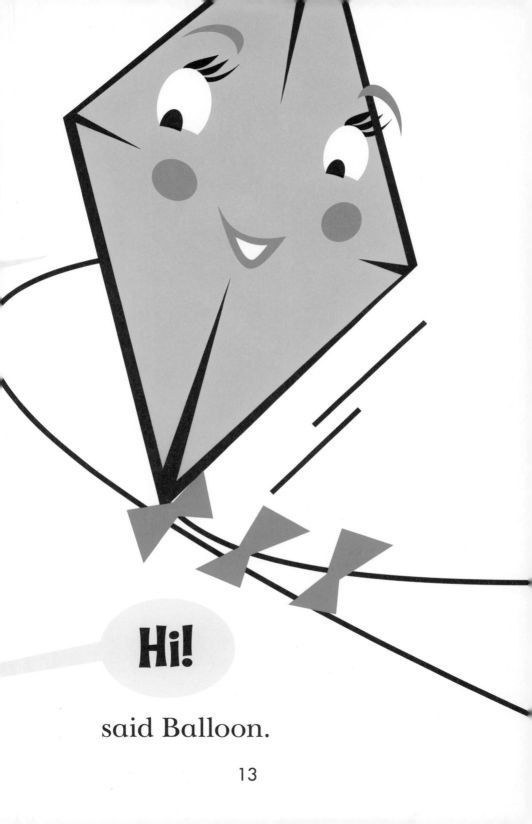

Hi!

said Balloon.

13

Balloon went up and up.

Wait for me! said Kite.

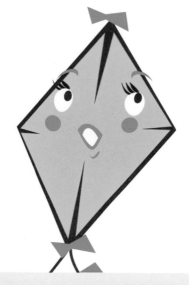

She pulled.

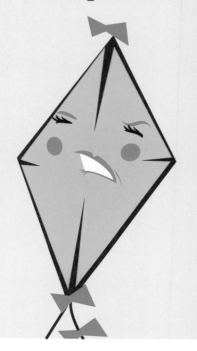

And she pulled.

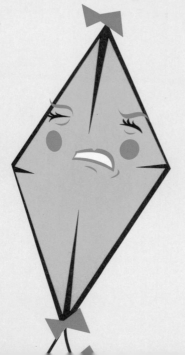

SNAP!

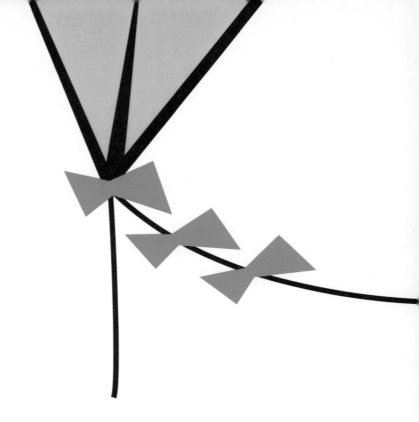

Until she was free.

At last they were side by side.

They flipped.

They dipped.

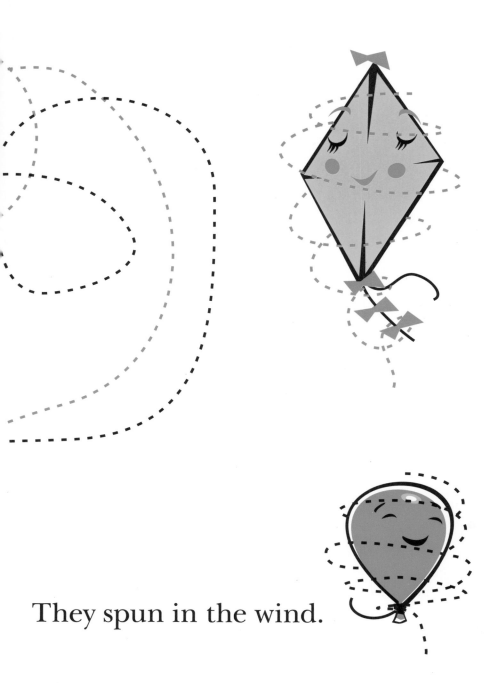

They spun in the wind.

They played in the cool clouds.

20

They rested in the warm sun.

It was all such fun.

Until the wind stopped blowing.

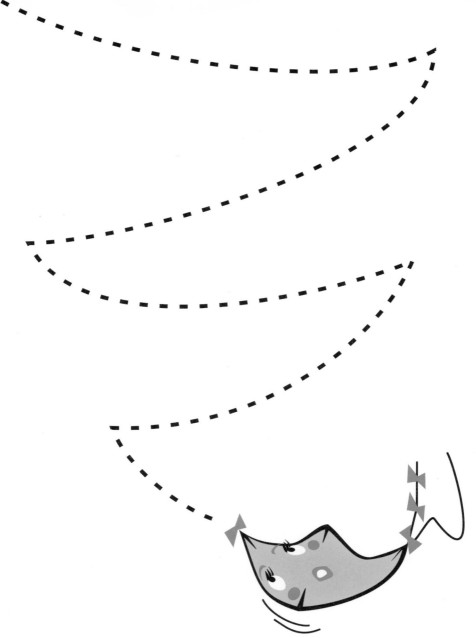

Down, down, down drifted Kite.

Down and down and down.

She landed in the branches
of a tall tree.

Balloon did not fall.

He kept going up.

Up and up and up.

He was so sad.

He missed his friend.

He did not see the bird.

And the bird did not see him.

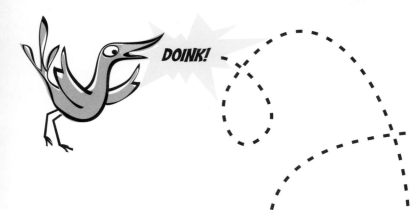

Down, down, down went Balloon.

Down and down and down.

It was such a long way down.

He was dizzy.

He was scared.

At last he landed.

PLOP!

31

And Kite was there to catch him.